MARY'S GAME

PENGUIN BOOKS

UK | USA | Canada | Ireland | Australia
India | New Zealand | South Africa | China

Penguin Random House Australia

Penguin Random House Australia is part of the Penguin Random House group of companies whose addresses can be found at global.penguinrandomhouse.com.

First published by Penguin, an imprint of
Penguin Random House Australia Pty Ltd, in 2026

Mary Fowler is exclusively represented by Josh White at Always Human.

Illustrations by Cate James
Cover and internal design by Tony Palmer © Penguin Random House Australia Pty Ltd
Cover background images: diagonal pattern Alona Khadzhyoglo/stock.adobe.com; netball pattern Martyshova/stock.adobe.com
Author photograph by Simon Upton
Typeset by Midland Typesetters, Australia

Printed and bound in Australia by Griffin Press, an accredited
ISO AS/NZS 14001 Environmental Management Systems printer

NATIONAL LIBRARY OF AUSTRALIA
A catalogue record for this book is available from the National Library of Australia

MIX
Paper | Supporting responsible forestry
FSC® C018684

ISBN 978 1 76135 621 6 (Paperback)

We at Penguin Random House Australia acknowledge that Aboriginal and Torres Strait Islander peoples are the Traditional Custodians and the first storytellers of the lands on which we live and work. We honour Aboriginal and Torres Strait Islander peoples' continuous connection to Country, waters, skies and communities. We celebrate Aboriginal and Torres Strait Islander stories, traditions and living cultures; and we pay our respects to Elders past and present.

MARY'S GAME

Mary Fowler

With Jasmin McGaughey
Illustrations by Cate James

PENGUIN BOOKS

CHAPTER ONE

My name is Maz! Well, my real name is Mary, but my mates call me Maz for short. I love having a nickname. When someone calls me Mary, I feel like I'm getting in trouble!

Today is Monday and I am

stepping through my school gates with something special I made on the weekend . . . something that is going to solve a big problem my friends and I have been having every lunchtime.

The problem?

The teachers have told us we are not allowed to do headers with the football anymore. Ms Ganier said, 'Hitting your head with that hard football is not good for your brain cells.'

'What are brain cells?' I asked her.

She gave me a serious look. 'The things in your brain that help you think and learn.'

'But my skull protects them!' I told her. 'And my mum said I have a very hard head.'

Ms Ganier smiled at me and said, 'I'm sure you do, Maz. But not everyone does. So, no headers at school, okay?'

'Okay,' I agreed, even though I didn't want to agree.

But now I am coming to school with a solution. I can't wait to show everyone!

A tea towel is covering the surprise, because I plan on doing a grand reveal.

I see my BFF by the bag racks and call out to her.

'Hey, Summer!'

Summer and I do *everything* together. We go to the beach together, we play cricket together in the holidays and we even get our hair cut together! My hair is brown and curly and loves to puff up, while Summer's hair is short and very, very straight.

'Hey, Maz,' Summer says as

she meets me at the front of our classroom. 'What's that?'

I grin, and my heart beats fast with excitement. 'I made it, Summer. You ready to see what it is?'

She nods and her eyes light up.

I pinch the tea towel. 'This weekend, Mum and I spent hours making a very special . . . um, thing. It's going to be so much fun.'

'Show me, Maz!' Summer says, waving her hands at me.

'Summer, this wasn't easy to make! I got glue everywhere – even on my backpack.'

'Not your backpack?' Summer gasps. She knows that my cow-shaped backpack is my most favourite thing that I own.

I'm wearing it now. I spin and show Summer that the backpack has been cleaned (thanks to Dad helping me) and that it is perfectly fine now.

'Come on, Maz, what is it?'

'Guess?' I say.

Summer rolls her eyes and puts her hands on her hips. 'Mary . . .'

Uh-oh, she said Mary instead of Maz. That's how I know she's serious!

'Okay, okay,' I say.

I pull the tea towel off like I am performing a magic trick, and Summer goes, 'Oohhh' and 'Ahhh' as I show her the paper football – sturdy but soft enough to not hurt our heads – I made.

It is the best!

CHAPTER TWO

'What is it made of?' Summer asks.

She gently takes the ball and bounces it on her fingertips.

'Paper, glue, water and flour,' I tell her.

'Flour?' She scrunches her face up like she doesn't believe me.

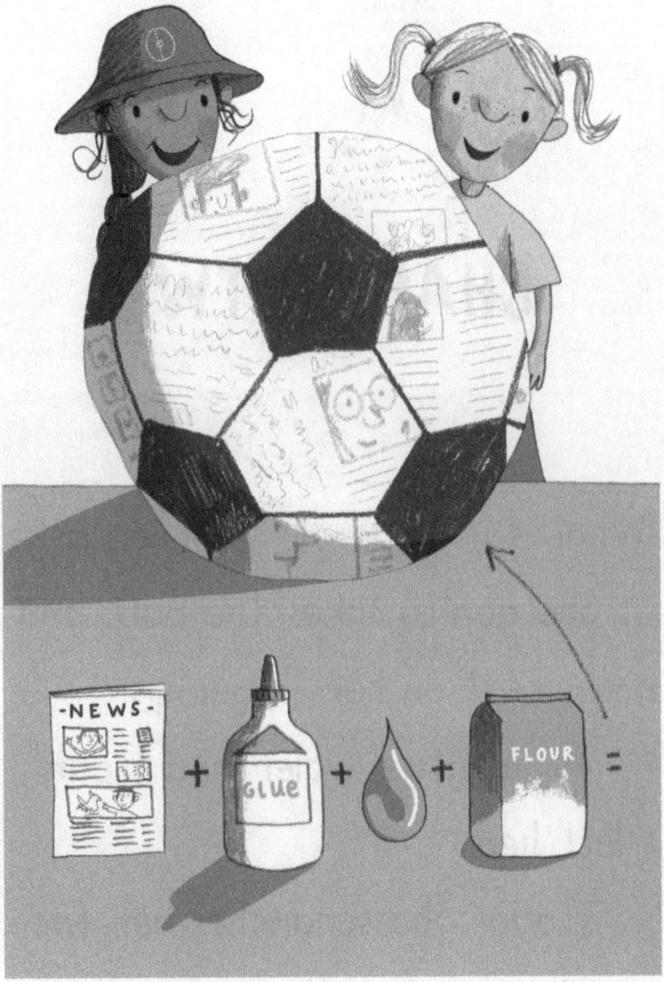
-NEWS-
GLUE
FLOUR

'Yup! And we blew up a ballon and put all the gooey mess on it to dry in this shape.'

Summer nods and I can tell she's impressed, which of course makes me extremely happy because I'm so proud of my paper football.

She hands it back and I juggle the ball with my legs to show her it's not too fragile. Juggling with your knees is hard work and it took me a long time practising to be able to do it.

'Oi, Maz, what's that?' Our friend

Mitaru comes along and puts his bag in the back rack.

Mitaru's name is pronounced with a 'the' sound in the middle, instead of a T sound. So – Mi-th-aru. He became my friend because I was the first person in our class to ask him how to pronounce his name correctly. Also because he loves playing sport outside just as much as Summer and I do.

'It's a football,' I tell him.

With my knee I bounce the ball to him and he catches it.

'You made this?' he says, looking closely at the swirls of paper. 'Is this newspaper?' he asks.

'It is! We had to go to the shops to buy it especially, since Mum and Dad just read the news on their phones.'

Mitaru juggles the ball a bit too and nods before handing it back.

'It means we can do headers at lunch!' I tell them.

Both Summer and Mitaru squeal and squeak.

'You're the best, Maz!'

'That's such a great idea!'

I put my bag on the bag rack and hold the ball safely under my arm as the rest of our class arrives. Most of them ask what it is I'm holding and *all* of them are excited to play football at lunchtime. I'm a little bit shier with everyone else who isn't Summer or Mitaru. So, I don't juggle the ball anymore. Instead, I let them all pass it around and look at it.

'Hello, everyone!' Ms Ganier arrives at the classroom door

with a big smile. 'Football away, Maz, class time now,' she says when the ball is passed to me.

'But Ms Ganier, can I bring it inside, please? It might melt in the sun!'

Ms Ganier takes a closer look at the ball and her eyes widen a little. 'That's a cool papier-mâché ball, Maz. All right, bring it inside. But no playing with it until lunch. You all have to be patient and wait.'

We all sigh. Waiting is no fun!

CHAPTER THREE

Waiting for lunch has never taken so long before!

I am in Year Two, which means my class is full of things to learn. Our desks are set up in rows facing a whiteboard. Our classroom is really colourful.

First up, we have a science lesson where Ms Ganier teaches us what soap does to germs. She puts pepper in a bowl of water and then drops a squirt of dishwashing soap into the water. The pepper shoots away like it is scared of the soap!

We have maths and then some reading time. My favourite part of the classroom is the reading corner. Picture this: the fluffiest, cosiest pile of pillows and two full bookcases holding everything you could want to read.

We also have a coat stand, where we put our library bags. When it's library time, Ms Ganier lets us take our bags so we can borrow books and take them home with us.

During class, my paper football sits on Ms Ganier's desk.

'How many headers do you think it will take before it breaks?' Summer asks me while Ms Ganier gets books from the back of the classroom.

Summer is sitting at the desk next to me. On my other side is Jazarah and in front of me is Anthony.

'I made it strong,' I tell her. 'But not strong enough to hurt.'

'Can we kick it?' Jazarah asks.

'Yes,' I tell her.

'Can we all play with you?' Anthony asks, swivelling in his seat. 'I love soccer.'

'It's called football,' I tell him. 'Not soccer.'

'It's called soccer,' Jazarah says and Anthony nods at me.

'Soccer is the round ball and footy is the oval ball. Right?' Anthony asks.

'It's called football!' I tell them again. 'Because that's what the people who invented it called it.'

Jazarah raises her eyebrows and Anthony nods his head.

Finally, after lots and lots of learning, it's time for recess!

Ms Ganier hands me the paper football. 'Be careful, Maz, okay?'

'I will, Ms Ganier. Thank you!'

I place the ball next to me while Summer, Mitaru and I eat

our snacks. Everyone who wants to play sits by us too, so they don't miss out.

When we're done, I hold the ball, put on my hat and lead the way to the oval!

CHAPTER FOUR

The sun is nice and warm today, so I bring my cool water bottle with me. Every night before bed I fill it up halfway with water and put it in the freezer. Then in the morning I fill the rest of it up with water and I have an icy cool drink for the whole school day.

'Careful, Maz,' Summer says. 'If your fingers are wet you might damage the football.'

'Oh no!'

She's right! I find a shady spot to put my water bottle and then

we all get down to business. The business of football!

'Can I go first, please?' Kema asks. She holds her hands under her chin and bounces on her toes. 'Please, please, Maz?'

'Okay,' I say. I hand her the ball and Kema stands with it between her fingers and her arms stretched.

She looks up to where she wants to throw the ball.

Bends her knees.

And throws it up!

The ball flies up into the

air and as it comes down, Kema shuffles her feet to stay underneath it. Then she bobs her head against it, so the ball flies up again.

She catches it with her hands this time when it comes down, and everybody cheers.

'Phew,' I whisper to Summer. 'I'm glad it really *is* strong enough.'

'You weren't sure?' she whispers back.

I shrug and focus back on the ball. Everyone is taking turns doing a header now. In fact, we end up playing hot potato with it.

Kema bounces it to Anthony, who bounces it to Jazarah, who bounces it to Mitaru. Then Mitaru is about to bounce it to Summer, but he stumbles and the ball falls!

It rolls away from our group until someone else on the oval

stops it with their foot and picks it up.

It's Ace, the best football player in Year Three!

'Over here, Ace!' Mitaru shouts, waving his arm.

Ace spots us all and walks over.

'Who made this?' he asks when he's standing in our circle.

'Maz did!' Summer says.

'That's pretty cool, Maz,' Ace says.

'It's so we can do headers without getting hurt,' I tell him. 'Do you want to have a go?'

Ace juggles the paper ball on his knees for a moment and his school hat flops around.

We know each other because we play football at the same club on Saturdays. Ace is a really good player because he's quick. I think I'm a good player because I like dribbling and dodging other players. I'm pretty good at figuring out what the players on the opposite team will do *before* they do it.

'You're playing headers?' Ace asks with an odd smile on his face.

'Yep!' I say.

He holds the ball out to me. 'How about instead of that, we play a full football game. Year Threes versus Year Twos?'

'Ooooh,' everyone says.

Nerves flip flop in my tummy. The Year Threes are fast and tall. But I love a challenge.

'You're on!'

CHAPTER FIVE

Ace calls all his friends over and we set up the goals. Since the older kids in Years Five and Six are using the actual football nets, we mark our goals with water bottles under the shade of the trees.

Two water bottles mark one goal, and two water bottles mark the other.

'Who will be referee?' Kema asks. 'Not me!'

'Not me either,' Ace says.

'Or me!'

'Or me!'

'Me either!'

I huff and put my hands on my hips. 'We don't need a ref, we'll all play fair, okay?'

Everyone nods and then we get into position.

Ace hands me the paper ball

and I place it in the middle of our field.

'Game ends when the bell rings?' Ace suggests.

'Got it,' I say.

He holds his hand out to me like professional football players do when they are the team captains. They shake hands to show everyone that they respect each other and the teams.

I feel sort of happy that Ace wants to shake my hand. I think it means he is taking us seriously even though my team is younger and smaller than his.

I shake his hand.

'Let's play!' Ace shouts.

And then we begin.

Ace starts by lightly tapping the paper ball. But he taps it too lightly to pass to his teammate, so I intercept it.

'You don't have to be afraid, Ace,' I tell him as I dribble. 'It's strong enough to kick.'

I move the ball down the field quickly and I hear my friends cheering. I see that Mitaru is open, so I kick the paper ball to him. It gains height and almost floats in the air.

Mitaru looks around him and then bends his knees.

He's going to do a header.

The first papier-mâché header of the game!

We all watch and wait and . . . success! The ball bounces off Mitaru's head and soars high into the sky like it wants to high-five the clouds.

Luckily, Mitaru aimed the ball towards Summer. Summer gently knocks the ball with her knee to slow it down. Then she quickly starts dribbling towards the goal.

Now, everyone has got over the shock that the ball works

normally. Ace's team spring into action. And they are *fast*.

One tall girl whose name I can't remember shoots up beside Summer and tackles it off her. They are a tangle of arms and legs and then Ace's team has the ball. Summer's face goes red just like I know it does whenever she's mad.

'It's okay!' I tell her. 'We've got this.'

My team manages to get the ball back and still no one has scored a goal. Jazarah gets it next, and she looks up as two bigger Year Threes charge towards her. She glances around and when she spots me, free and open, she grins.

'Maz!' she shouts. 'Here!'

Jazarah kicks the paper ball. Except, she kicks it hard.

I know she's used to playing AFL, so maybe that's why the ball doesn't fly towards me, it flies *up*!

We all tilt our heads to watch it.

'Oh no,' I say.

There's nothing we can do but watch as the ball bounces onto a tree branch and wedges itself there.

The paper ball is stuck in a tree!

CHAPTER SIX

'I'm so sorry, Maz!' Jazarah says. Her eyes are glassy like she might cry.

'It's okay,' I tell her. 'We'll get it down. And if we don't, we'll figure it out. We can make an even better one.'

She nods but still looks a little worried.

'How are we going to get it down?' Summer asks as she stands next to me.

Some of the Year Threes have run off now that the ball is stuck, but Ace stays.

Ace turns to me. 'How about . . .'

BRINNNNG!

The bell is ringing.

'Oh no!' Jazarah says. 'There's no time to get it down.'

'It's perfect,' I tell her. 'Now we

can figure out *how* we'll do it. We can meet back here at lunchtime?'

'Sure,' Ace says. 'See you all then.'

When we get back to the classroom, I'm happy that Ms Ganier has turned the air-conditioning on, so the room is nice and cool.

'Goodness, don't you all look sweaty,' she says when we sit in our seats.

'Oh Ms Ganier, I kicked the ball too high and it got stuck in a tree!' Jazarah says. 'The ball Maz made.'

'It's okay, Jazarah.' I pat her shoulder and Ms Ganier smiles at me, which makes me feel good. 'We're going to try to get it down at lunchtime,' I say.

'And if you can't, we can ask the groundskeepers for some help,' Ms Ganier says. 'Can anyone think of how we might get a ball down from a tree?' she asks the whole class.

Kema raises her hand. 'A leaf blower?'

'That's a good idea, Kema,' Ms Ganier says. 'Any other ideas?'

'Climb it?' someone asks.

'It's too tall,' Summer answers.

'Throw something to knock it down?' Anthony suggests. 'Like a shoe?'

'Nobody should be taking their shoes off,' Ms Ganier says. 'Have a think about a *safe* way we could get it down, okay? And while you're doing that, we're going to start on our journals. Everyone, take out your notebook and pencil . . .'

Ms Ganier loves getting us to write down what we did over the weekend or what we played at recess. She says writing can help us work out problems.

I'm not too worried about the stuck ball. I had so much fun making it on the weekend that

I would love to make another one. But I see that Jazarah still looks sad. She keeps giving me guilty looks – puppy-dog eyes, Mum would call it. Her eyes make me feel all sorry inside and like I want to make things better.

I need to think of a way to get that ball down.

CHAPTER SEVEN

By the time the bell rings for lunchtime, the class has come up with lots of ideas. The ideas are:

1. Mitaru and Anthony climbing the tree.
2. Summer standing on my shoulders to reach the ball.

3. Kema and Jazarah asking the groundkeepers for a leaf blower.

And me? Well, I have one idea, and it involves a *real* football that I take from our bucket of sports equipment.

We head outside, where we meet Ace under the tree.

'Well, it's still there,' Kema says.

'It looks cosy,' Summer says.

She's right. The ball looks tucked away in the branch, surrounded by leaves like it's sitting in a nest.

'Maybe a bird will come along and help us,' Ace says.

'Come on,' I say to them all. 'Who wants to try first?' I clap my hands and smile. We may not be able to play with the paper ball, but we can still have fun!

'Me!' Anthony says. 'I'm climbing. Mitaru, will you be my spotter?'

'I have a bad feeling about this,' I say.

Anthony and Mitaru walk up to the tree and talk to one another for a moment before getting into position.

Anthony stretches his arms and legs.

Mitaru hovers next to him with his hands out, ready to catch Anthony if he falls. The trunk of the tree is really wide, so

Anthomy spreads his arms out like he's going to give it a hug.

'Here we go,' he says.

Butterflies flutter in my tummy as I watch Anthony start to climb.

His arms reach up and he pulls his whole body up, his feet digging into the sides of the tree.

And then, he stops.

Anthony gasps. And then . . .

'Ahhhh!' Anthony yells in a warbling voice, gripping the tree tighter. 'I just realised I'm scared of heights!'

CHAPTER EIGHT

Athony is actually only about one metre off the ground. He's not even up that high!

'Anthony,' Ace says, 'you can let go.'

But Anthony has his eyes shut and is shaking his head.

Mitaru, who is still standing next to him, looks at us and shrugs. 'How come you didn't know you were afraid of heights?' Mitaru asks him.

'I've never had to climb a tree before,' Anthony says with his eyes still closed.

'I promise you'll be okay, Anthony,' I tell him. 'The ground is really close. Just let one foot down.'

Anthony's whole body is shaking now, and I feel bad for him. I step up close and put my hand on his arm. 'See?' I say. 'I'm right here.'

Anthony cracks open one eye to look at me. Then that eye swivels all the way down.

'Oh,' he says and lets go.

I wouldn't even call it a fall to the ground! But Anthony plomps down and dusts his hands on his pants. 'Well, that was scary.'

PLOMP

We all crack up at Anthony's smile. He's always good at making us laugh.

I pat him on the back. 'I'm just glad you're okay. Now, who's next?'

'I'll stand on your shoulders!' Summer says.

I bend down and Kema and Jazarah stand on either side of me to help Summer. They each hold one of her hands as she places her knees on my shoulders.

One knee.

Then the next knee.

I stand up straight and everyone goes, 'Whoa.'

'Okay, now get up onto your feet, Summer,' I say.

'I can't!' Summer hisses to me.

'Huh?' It's hard to hear her because her legs are pressing against my ears.

'I can't move, or I'll fall,' Summer says to me.

I try to look up at her, but she cries out and I see her arms windmilling from the corner of my eyes.

Jazarah and Kema reach out

and steady her, and I go still. I can't move. What if Summer falls!

'Mary! Summer!' someone shouts. 'Stop that now!' It's Ms Ganier.

Ms Ganier comes along and stops in front of me. 'Bend a little, Mary,' she says and then helps Summer carefully get down from my shoulders.

I know Ms Ganier is mad at me because she used my full name – Mary – instead of Maz. My cheeks get all warm as she frowns at us.

'That's not safe. No more standing on shoulders, okay?'

'Yes, Ms Ganier,' Summer and I say at the same time.

Ms Ganier leaves, shaking her head and muttering something that I don't hear. But I do catch my name and Summer's name and the word 'trouble'.

'What now?' Summer asks me.

'I have one more idea,' I say.

CHAPTER NINE

I get the real football and back up away from the tree.

'You're going to kick it down?' Ace asks.

'Yeah,' I say.

'But what if the paper football gets dented?'

'This is all my fault,' Jazarah says. 'I'm so sorry.'

'It's not that bad, Jazarah,' I tell her. 'Don't be sorry. Plus, I've had fun trying to get it down, so it doesn't matter if we dent it.'

'If we dent it, maybe we can turn it into something else?' Mitaru suggests. 'Like a bowl for chips?'

'Or a hat!' Kema says.

'Or a seat,' Anthony says. 'For when you have to sit on the grass?'

'Good ideas,' Ace says. 'But Maz, are you sure you can aim well enough?'

Ace is squinting up at the paper football. It's wedged in very tightly between the branch and the trunk. There are other branches and leaves in the way of it too.

'I'm sure,' I tell him. 'And if I can't, everyone else can have a go too.'

My friends stand behind and watch me put the ball on the grass.

I take a few steps back. I look at where I want the ball to go.

Step.

Step.

Kick!

The shiny black-and-white football zooms through the air and hits the paper ball directly!

'Score!' Summer shouts and everyone else cheers too.

We run over to where both footballs have landed.

'Is it broken?' Jazarah asks. 'Is it dented?'

Ace picks up the real football and I pick up the paper one. I spin it around in my fingers looking for anything that could be wrong.

Nothing is dented or ripped or broken at all.

'It's completely okay,' I tell them all. 'We did it!'

CHAPTER TEN

The bell rings pretty soon after we rescue the ball and we all walk back to the classrooms. Ace pauses outside the Year Three block.

'I had fun! Thanks for making the ball, Maz!' He waves and all of us Year Twos wave back.

'He's so cool,' Mitaru says.

'I want to be that cool when I'm in Year Three,' Kema says.

I look at the ball in my hands. 'Hey, Jazarah?'

She turns her head to look at me. I gently kick the ball towards her. 'Here, you can keep it,' I say.

Jazarah's big brown eyes get even bigger. 'Really?' she asks.

'Yeah!' I say. 'I had so much fun making it that I kind of want to make it again.'

Summer slings her arm around

my shoulders. 'Can you make me one too?'

'Or you could try something new,' Anthony suggests. 'Like a paper handball?'

'Or a paper basketball!' Jazarah suggests, bouncing the football between her fingertips.

'Um, I don't think you all understand how paper works,' I tell them. 'It's not very bouncy. But I'll give it a go!'

We walk back to class together.

I'm sweaty and tired, but I've

had so much fun with my friends that I can't wait for play time tomorrow!

ABOUT MARY FOWLER

Mary Fowler is one of Australia's most exciting footballers and a rising global icon of the game.

She made her international debut for the Matildas when she was 15 and has performed on the world's biggest stages, including the FIFA Women's World Cup at home in Australia and the Olympics in Tokyo and Paris.

Her blend of technical brilliance, creativity, power and versatility has seen her shine for both the Matildas and Manchester City.

With her Papua New Guinean and Irish heritage shaping both her game and her outlook on life, Mary Fowler embodies a new generation of athletes redefining the sport – authentic, gifted and inspiring on and off the pitch.

Look out for more stories with Mary Fowler!

